THE CLASSIC POEM FROM
LEWIS CARROLL'S
THROUGH THE LOOKING-
GLASS, AND WHAT
ALICE FOUND THERE

REIMAGINED AND ILLUSTRATED BY
CHRISTOPHER
MYERS

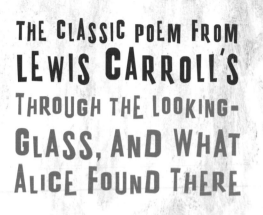

JABBERWOCKY

JUMP AT THE SUN

HYPERION BOOKS FOR CHILDREN
NEW YORK

'TWAS BRILLIG, AND THE SLITHY TOVES DID GYRE AND GIMBLE IN THE WABE: ALL MIMSY WERE THE BOROGOVES, AND THE MOME RATHS OUTGRABE.

"Beware the Jabberwock, my son!

THE JAWS THAT BITE, THE CLAWS THAT CATCH!

BewAre the JubJub Bird, aNd shUN THE FrumioUS BaNDErsNatCh!"

He took his vorpal SWORD IN HAND;

Long time the manxome foe he SOUGHT—

SO RESTED HE BY THE TUMTUM TREE,

AND STOOD AWHILE IN THOUGHT.

And, as in uffish thought he stood, The **JABBERWOCK**, with eyes of **FLAME**,

Came **WHIFFLING** through the tulgey wood, And **BURBLED** as it came!

AND WITH ITS HEAD
HE WENT GALUMPHING
BACK.

"AND HAST THOU SLAIN
THE JABBERWOCK?

COME TO MY ARMS,
MY BEAMISH BOY!

O FRABJOUS DAY!
CALLOOH! CALLAY!"

HE CHORTLED IN HIS JOY.

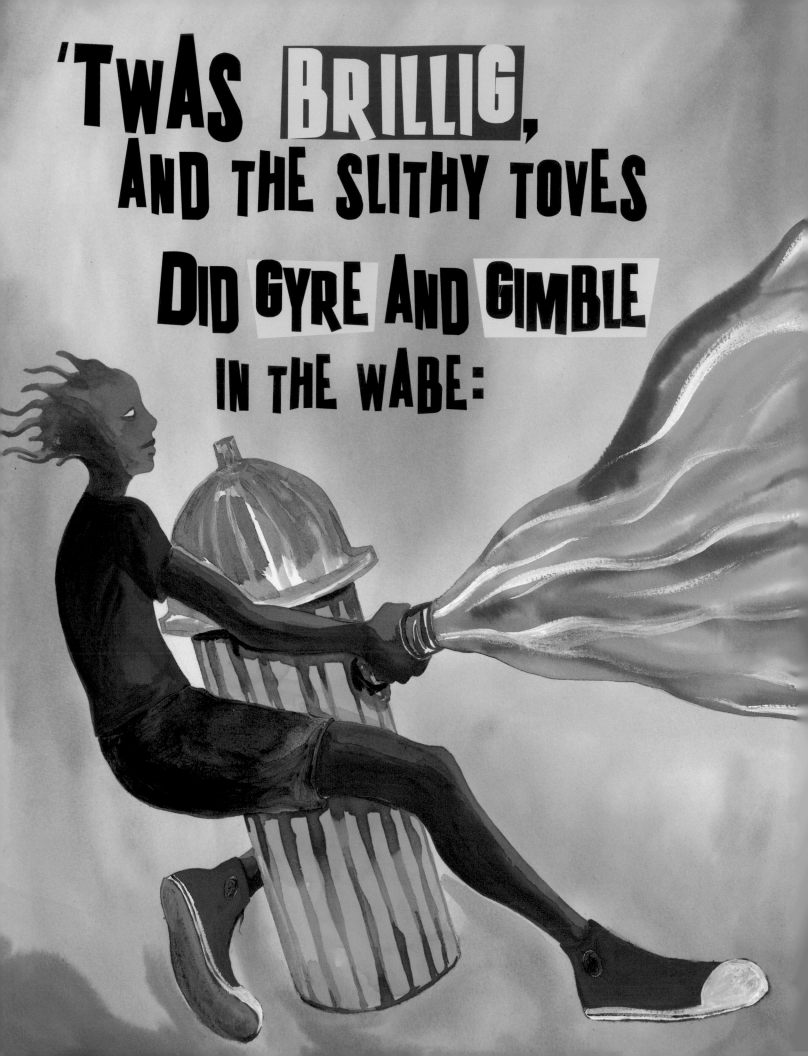

ALL **MIMSY** WERE
THE BOROGOVES,

AND THE MOME RATHS
OUTGRABE.

A Short Note on the Origins of this Book

Although Children's Books are thought to be the products of wild imaginations and unfettered flights of fancy, my books are, more often than not, products of painstaking research. This version of *Jabberwocky* is no different. I had originally intended to create a picture book entitled *A Short History of Gibberish, Gobbledygook, and Assorted Yang*, an exploration of nonsense language through the ages. No study of the nonsensical would be complete without thorough investigation of the famous poem by Charles Lutwidge Dodgson. I pored over the nine extant volumes of his diaries, now in the safekeeping of the British Library.

It was through happenstance or luck that in the eighth volume of his journal I spied a curious note in the margin, the single word *ollamalitzli*. . . . It refers to an ancient Mesoamerican game of religious and ritual significance played by several cultures, including the Olmecs and Aztecs. The object of the game was to manipulate a rubber ball through a stone hoop affixed high on a wall. Dodgson surely had read about the game, much the same way that James Naismith, "inventor" of basketball, had read about it, in one of the many missionary journals that were popular in that day, especially among doctors of divinity (which both men were). Clearly, a basic familiarity with this nascent form of basketball is central to understanding the work.

I would be remiss not to acknowledge the assistance of several noted members of the Lewis Carroll Society (LCS), especially Sagal Abshir (LCS-Mogadishu), Shadra Strickland (LCS-Bed-Stuy), Wei Weng (LCS-Nanning), Micheline Brown (LCS-Oslo), Namrata Tripathi and Elizabeth Clark (LCS-New York), and Shilpi Gupta (LCS-Kashmir).

While Dodgson himself published several fanciful accounts of the meaning of his poem, I believe these to be sheer obfuscation, on a par with the coded writing of other noted polymaths, such as Leonardo da Vinci or Jaber ibn Hayyan (a noted eighth-century alchemist, whose name provides the etymology for the word *gibberish* and perhaps some inspiration for the titular beast of the poem). Even some of the so-called nonsense words used in the piece are more reminiscent of Nahuatl (the Aztec language) terms of exhortation used on the proto-basketball field. *Calaqui*, the Nahuatl word meaning "to come inside/get in," is highly reminiscent of "Callooh! Callay!" for example.

Dodgson's persistent interests in missionary work, in sport as a moral battleground, and in language serve to shed much light on what I had previously thought of as simply a charming children's verse. As always, a bit of time spent in a library has opened new worlds of understanding for me, and has enriched the nonsense that I can share with whole new generations.

—Christopher Myers

Text by Lewis Carroll · Illustrations copyright © 2007 by Christopher Myers

Library of Congress Cataloging-in-Publication Data on file. · Reinforced binding
ISBN-13: 978-1-4231-0372-1 · ISBN-10: 1-4231-0372-6

Visit www.jumpatthesun.com